W9-CUT-825

WITHDRAWN FROM LIBRARY
Soiled, Worn or Obsolete

THE PEOPLE ZOO

by
GEORGE PRICE

Words by Stephen Josephs

Windmill Books

New York

In homage to Walt Whitman
                    G.P.

"I think I could turn and live with the animals,
They are so peaceful and self-contain'd."

                              Walt Whitman

All rights reserved
including the right of reproduction
in whole or in part in any form.

Text Copyright © 1971 by Stephen Josephs
Illustrations Copyright © 1971 by George Price
'Windmill Books' and the colophon
accompanying it are a trademark of
Windmill Books, Inc., registered in
the United States Patent Office.

Published by Windmill Books, Inc.
257 Park Avenue South
New York, New York 10010
An Intext Publisher

First Printing

ISBN 0-87807-034-6 Trade
ISBN 0-87807-035-4 Library
Library of Congress Catalog Card Number LC 74-159158

Manufactured in the United States of America
Published on the same day in Canada by Abelard-
Schuman Canada Limited

Designed by Cathy M. Altholz

The People Zoo

The Zoo's a cool and noisy place
More fitting for the human race
Than for us beasts, thought Ancient Ape.

On this thought, so introspected,
Younger apes reflected
And, gave the plan effective shape.

In caucus, birds of different feather
Raucously flocked together
And agreed, by fair election,

(So did other furry folk
Who thought it more than just a joke)
—To subvert natural selection.

As a cure for social ills
Without recourse to shrinks or pills,
To offer hope for absolution

Without evangelists or leaders,
Yogi, yoga, or special pleaders,
To stop (at least *confine*) pollution—

All the *humans*
(me and you)
would be the inmates
of the Zoo.

—A satisfactory conclusion.

With good humor, nay, elation,
The beasts provided transportation,
Animal hunter, hunted man.

By air and sea the chase went on.
The prey, but slightly woebegone,
Cooperated, never ran.

Thus all the humans
(me and you)
became stars of
The People Zoo.

Outside the bars the beasts reflect
On the almost animal intellect.

Inside the cages, plumage wild
Of modern woman, man, and child.

Oddities perform their drill
On a beast-attended concrete hill.

What joy—at first—to see them play
What fun—at first—to see the way

They paw and sniff around each other,
Greeting her as "friend" and him as "brother."

What peaceful folk, and so benign!
Their mannerisms so refined.

Yet, as they watched the folk display
Themselves, and, closer, saw the way

They chose up sides for lethal games
And called each other hateful names,

Put on disguise, searched out some hex,
The whole affair was rated X.

"Too much for us!" the viewers sighed.
"Unfit for baby beasts," they cried.

"A great idea—but out of hand.
Such beasts, *we* beasts can't understand."

"Too much to bear! Too sad to see!
Let's set these awful creatures free!"

And so they did.
Then ran and hid.